Goodnight Already!

Jory John & Benji Davies

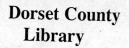

First published in hardback by HarperCollins Children's Books,
a division of HarperCollins Publishers, USA, in 2015
First published in hardback in Great Britain by HarperCollins Children's Books in 2015
First published in paperback in 2015

1 3 5 7 9 10 8 6 4 2

ISBN: 978-0-00-810135-0

HarperCollins Children's Books is a division of HarperCollins Publishers Ltd.

Text copyright © Jory John 2015
Illustrations copyright © Benji Davies 2015

Typography by Jeanne L. Hogle

Visit our website at: www.harpercollins.co.uk

Printed and bound in China

To my mom, Deborah John, a bear enthusiast,
who continually reminds me to get enough sleep.
And also to my friend and agent Steven Malk,
who starts sending me numerous text
messages around midnight. And to Alyssa, always.
—Jory John

This book is for Nina. Thank you
for the insomnia-induced inspiration
that started this story. And thanks also
to Kirsten, who orchestrated
the whole shebang.
—Benji Davies

"I've never been so tired. I could sleep for weeks. Months, even!"

"I've never been so awake. I wonder what ol' Bear's up to?"

"I can't wait to sleep. Here we go . . . yes. . ."

"Bear! It's me!
Duck! Open up!
C'mon, buddy!"

"Talk all night?"

"No."

"Play cards?"

"You already said that."

"Read books to each other?"

"No."

"Whatever."

"Fine. Goodnight already."

"Ahh. Bed. Yes."

"Almost . . . asleep . . ."

"Psst! Bear! It's Duck! From next door!"

"**What?!**"

"I want to make cookies.
Can I borrow some sugar?"

"**No.**"

"Butter?"

"**No.**"

"Dough?"

"No."

"Salt?"

"No."

"Butter?"

"You already said that."

"Can I just borrow some cookies then?"

"No."

"Goodnight already!"

"That duck . . . always bothering me! . . .
I need to get some new neighbours. . .

. . . Later, though . . . too tired . . .
must sleep."

"**How on earth . . . ?!**"
"I used my spare key."
"**That was for emergencies!**"
"This *is* an emergency."

"**What?**
What is it, Duck?
What's the emergency?**"

"I stubbed my beak. See?"

"Duck! You've got to stop waking me up.

out! NOW!"

"But..."

"I SAID GOODNIGHT ALREADY!"

"Bear is so grumpy! His bad attitude is making me tired."

"Once upon a time there was a . . . there was a . . ."

"I've never been so awake."